The Great Show-and-Tell Disaster

To my buddy
COLTON PAUL !

Mike Reiss

To MY DEAR and DREAMY wife —
M. R.

To my family—love —
M. C.

Designed by Debbie Guy-Christiansen

Published by Price Stern Sloan, a division of Penguin Putnam Books for Young Readers,
345 Hudson Street, New York, NY 10014
Published simultaneously in Canada. Printed in Hong Kong.

Library of Congress Cataloging-in-Publication Data

Reiss, Mike.
   The great show-and-tell disaster / written by Mike Reiss ; illustrated by Mike Cressy.
      p. cm.
   Summary: Desperate to bring something exciting to show-and-tell at school, Ned invents a
Mix-up Ray and causes a commotion when Cathy becomes a yacht, the school bus becomes
a sub, and his teacher, Mrs. Eton, becomes a monster.
   ISBN 0-8431-7680-6
   [1. Schools—Fiction. 2. Show-and-tell presentations—Fiction. 3. Anagrams—Fiction.
4. Humorous stories. 5. Stories in rhyme.] Title: Great show-and-tell disaster. II. Cressy, Mike, ill. III. Title.

PZ8.3.R277   Gr 2001
[E]—dc21   2001021011

ISBN 0-8431-7680-6   A B C D E F G H I J

The Great Show-and-Tell Disaster

By Mike Reiss • Illustrated by Mike Cressy

PSS!
PRICE STERN SLOAN

There once was a young inventor named Ned.
He was lying in bed, and he wished he were dead.
Show-and-Tell was this morning, and—wouldn't you know?
He had nothing to tell and nothing to show.
He'd already brought in his toad and his turtle,
His bronze baby shoes and his Aunt Myrtle's girdle,
His tonsils, appendix, his dinosaur fossil—
Ned needed something completely colossal!

He went to his closet and dug out his stash
Of valuable treasures he'd found in the trash:
A rusty eggbeater, a toy laser beam,
A handheld electronic spelling machine.
A Slinky with kinks and an old ping-pong paddle,
A snow globe that said "Having Fun in Seattle."
He smushed them together with duct tape and glue.
He had an invention, but what did it do?

He cranked the contraption,
the laser glowed red.
He pointed the beam
at a shoe on the bed.
With a flash, the old SHOE
had turned into a HOSE,
That sprayed ice-cold water
on Ned's books and clothes!
Then Ned zapped his LAMP,
it turned into a PALM!
He took a deep breath
and he tried to stay calm:

"I'll call my invention . . . Ned's Mix-up Ray!
I'll be rich! I'll be famous! Or at least get an 'A'!"

He ran down to breakfast to tell Dad and Mom
That his shoe was a hose and his lamp was a palm.
"My newest invention makes normal stuff weird!
It lets a CAT ACT, and makes BREAD grow a BEARD!"

But just then the laser beam bounced off a dish,
Changing his AUNT to a big TUNA fish!
"Oops, sorry!" said Ned, and he ran off to school,
While his Mom and his Dad put his aunt in the pool.

On his way, Ned passed by Mr. Clemens, the grocer.
Did he leave the store as he found it? Oh, no sir!
Old Mr. Clemens saw, after a while,
That his PEAS were now APES and his LIMES learned to SMILE.

His LEMONS were MELONS, his MELONS were LEMONS.
"Eh, what's the difference," said old Mr. Clemens.
Then Ned went too far—he made every PEACH CHEAP.
And old Mr. Clemens said, "Beat it, you creep!"

At school, Show-and-Tell started out pretty slow—
Cathy brought mustard. And Gary—a hoe.

But things got exciting when Ned's Mix-up Ray
Made CATHY a YACHT and turned GARY to GRAY!
Jane Keene and Jane Greene were both meaner than mean,
But this bad pair of JANES made a nice pair of JEANS.
He made BRIAN a BRAIN, with a big throbbing thinker,
Changed NAT to an ANT and made KRISTEN a STINKER!

Then Ned went too far—MRS. ETON, the teacher,
Turned into a MONSTER—a three-headed creature!

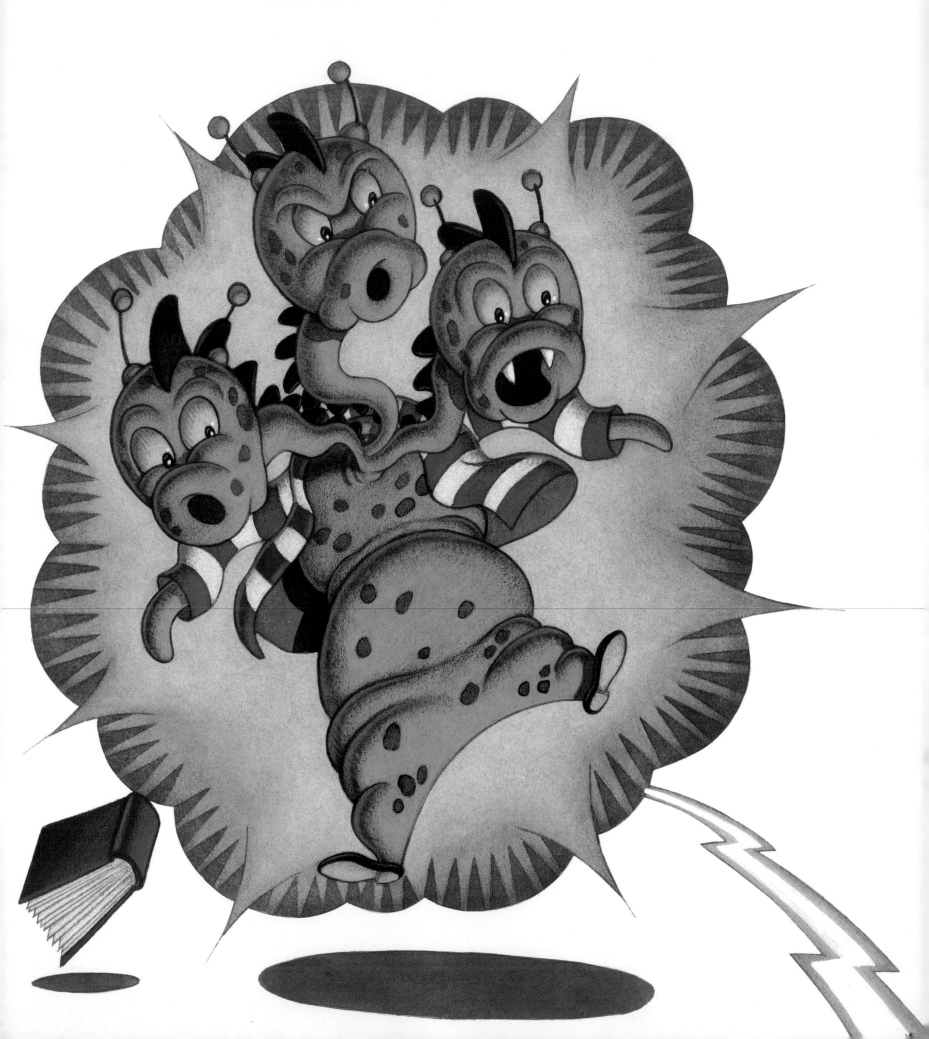

"Ned," roared the teacher, "you get an F-plus!"
Then she hustled the children outside to a bus.
"It's time for our trip to the Museum of Art.
And I'm warning you, Ned, don't try anything smart.
I have six eyes and they're watching you, Bub."
But she hadn't noticed the BUS was a SUB.

They sailed through the city. Ned zapped every sign.
Look very closely—can you find all nine?

STORE

SALE

PLAY HOUSE

CATS

COLA

GAS

GAS

GERMANY

STOP

ELM ST.

SLOW

At the Museum of Art, Ned roamed through the halls,
Making PIECRUST from PICTURES that hung on the walls.

He changed ART to a RAT, he turned ART into TAR.
One BUST was the STUB of a smelly cigar.
An URN sprouted legs and went out for a RUN.
And nine NEON sculptures had dwindled to NONE.

Out in the courtyard, surrounded by trees,
Rodin's *THE KISS* had turned into *THE SKIS*.
And sitting on top, where a PIGEON would perch.
ONE PIG was squealing, and left in the lurch.
A giant DOG statue replaced a Greek GOD,
His THRONE was a HORNET (which looked rather odd!).
Ned made a mess out of each masterpiece,
And trashed all the treasures of classical Greece.

When she saw the madness throughout the museum,
The teacher let loose with a three-headed scream.
And suddenly Ned knew this wasn't a game.
Things were a NIGHTMARE without the RIGHT NAME!

Cathy the yacht said, "You wrecked Show-and-Tell!"
Kristen the stinker sobbed, "You made me smell!"
Brian the brain asked, "Have you lost your mind?"
The urn with the legs kicked him in the behind.
The MOOD wasn't good, and poor Ned could sense DOOM,
So he ran and he hid in the little boys' room.

"I've scrambled my friends and the whole art collection,"
Ned thought as he stared at his gloomy reflection.
Then Ned had a brainstorm! He knew it could work!
"I'm a genius!" he cried. "And, well . . . kind of a jerk."

He aimed at the mirror with NED'S MIX-UP RAY.
The device zapped itself . . . and became UNMIXED SPRAY!

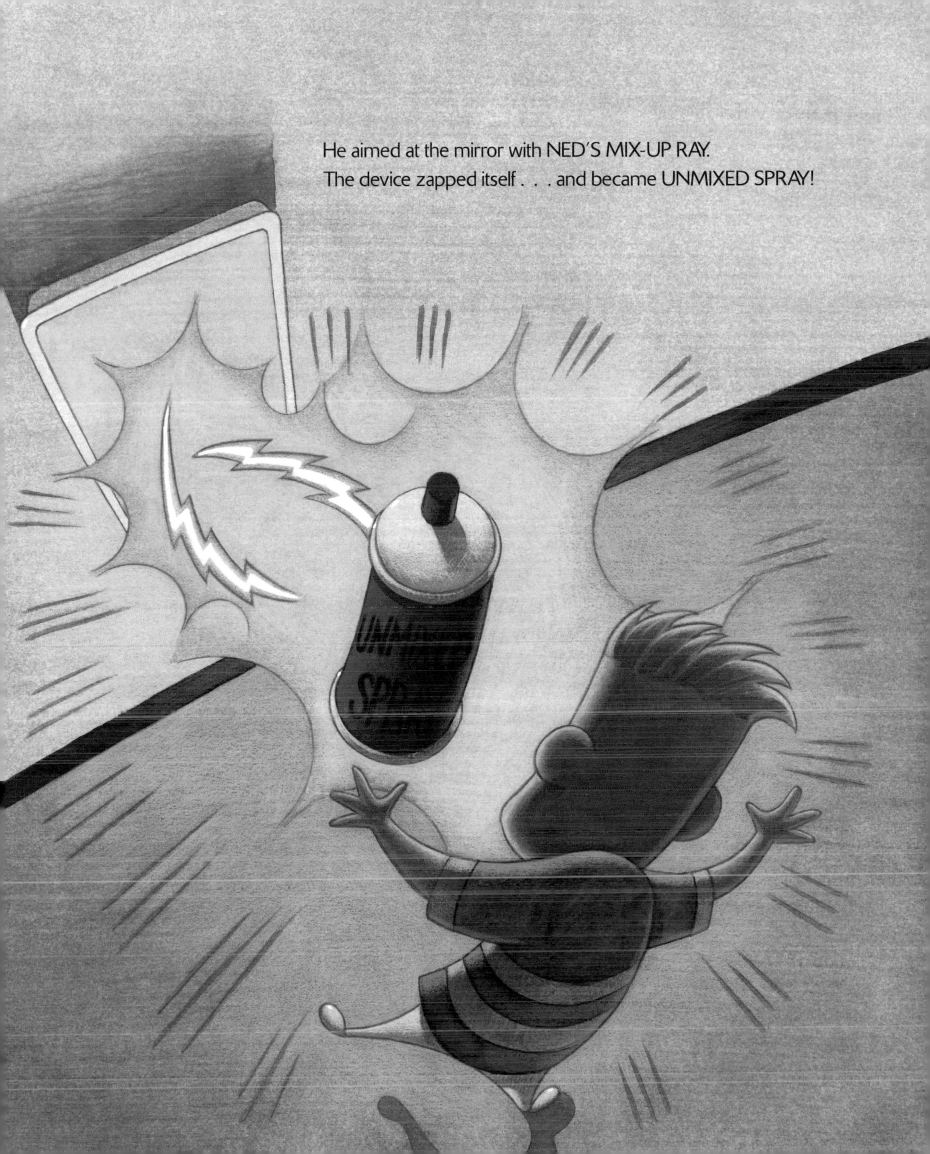

With a spritz of his spray, he made ART from a RAT.
The YACHT became CATHY, the ANT became NAT.
BRIAN's huge BRAIN was tucked back in his cranium.
KRISTEN the STINKER smelled like a geranium.
The only thing left was the three-headed creature.
This monster was scary, but so was his teacher.

Ned sprayed and the MONSTER became MRS. ETON.
She was angry at first, then she started to sweeten:
"Ned, you have been a most mischievous kid,
But I think you've undone all the damage you did.
And you kept this from being another dull day,
So I'm raising your grade from F-plus to an 'A'."

On his way home from school he stopped by the store,
And found things were better than they'd been before.
"Those PAGERS are selling much better than GRAPES,"
Mr. Clemens explained, "so I hired the apes
To work as my clerks. They have excellent manners.
The best part of all is they work for bananas!
You've helped me a lot—you're a very bright child."
Mr. Clemens and Ned (and all the limes) smiled.

Ned returned home feeling proud of himself,
And he set down the spray with his "A" on the shelf.
He'd fixed all the problems at home and at school,
(Except for his aunt, who is *still* in the pool!).
But what should he bring to the next Show-and-Tell?
A bell? Or a shell? Or a stale caramel?
Or he might build a Switcheroo Gizmo instead . . . !
But for now it's the END of the story of NED.